Jorge Luis Borges
The Lottery in Babylon

Translated by Norman Thomas di Giovanni

ERIS
gems

LIKE ALL MEN IN BABYLON, I HAVE been a proconsul; like all, a slave. I have known absolute power, public disgrace, and imprisonment. Behold, my right forefinger is missing. Behold, beneath this rent in my cloak my flesh bears a red tattoo. It is a beth, the second letter of our alphabet. On nights when the moon is full, this symbol grants me sway over men whose sign is a gimel but, at the same time, it makes me subject to those marked with an aleph. They, on moonless nights, owe obedience to men branded with the gimel. In the twilight of dawn, before a black altar deep in a vault, I have slit the throats of sacred bulls. For the space of a lunar year, I was declared invisible. When I cried out, no one answered; when I stole bread, I was not beheaded. I have suffered that which the Greeks did not—uncertainty. In a bronze chamber, confronting the strangler's silent cord, hope did not abandon me; in the river of pleasure, neither did panic. Heraclides of Pontus relates in wonder that Pythagoras remembered having been Pyrrhus and before that Euphorbus and before that some other mortal. In order to remember similar experiences, I have no need to fall back either on death or deception.

I owe this almost hideous alternation in my fortunes to a practice that other republics do not follow or that in them works in an imperfect, secret way. I speak of our lottery. Although I have not delved into its history, I find our sages cannot agree on it. Of the lottery's mighty purpose, I know what a man unversed in astrology knows of the moon. I come from a bewildering country, where daily life revolves round the lottery. Until now, I have given this institution no more thought than I have the behaviour of the inscrutable gods or of my own heart. Here, far from Babylon and its cherished customs, I think back in amazement on the lottery and on the blasphemous speculations about it whispered by men lurking in shadows.

My father used to say that long ago—was it centuries? years?—the Babylonian lottery was little more than a street game. He said (I do not know how true it is) that barbers sold for a few copper coins oblong bits of bone or parchment, marked with symbols. A draw was made in broad daylight, and, without further complication, winners received a handful of silver coins. It was, as you see, a simple arrangement.

Of course, these so-called lotteries failed. Their moral force was nil. They did not take into account all of man's capacities but only his hope. Faced with public apathy, the shopkeepers who set up these venal lotteries began to lose money. One of their number, introducing a reform, added a few forfeits to the winning lots. Accordingly, anyone who bought a numbered ticket faced a twofold contingency—that of winning a sum of money or of paying a fine. These fines were often considerable. Naturally, the slight risk—out of every thirty winning numbers one was unlucky—aroused the public's interest. The Babylonians threw themselves into the game. Anyone who did not buy a ticket was looked on as a coward and a faintheart. In time, this well-deserved contempt grew. Those who did not play were despised, but so were the losers, who had to pay the fine. The Company (as it then began to be called) had to protect the winners, who could not collect their prizes until almost all the fines were in the lottery's coffers. Claims would be made against the losers, and a judge would order them to pay the fine, together with court costs, or spend a few days in jail. To cheat the Company, the losers all chose jail. Out of this defiance by a few the Company's absolute power, its ecclesiastical and metaphysical basis, was born.

Soon after, financial reports gave up listing the fines and took to publishing only the number of days in custody a particular ticket imposed. The omission, which passed almost unnoticed at the time, proved to be of prime importance. It was the first appearance in the lottery of a non-pecuniary element. Success was immediate. On the insistence of the gamblers, the Company found it had to issue more unlucky numbers.

Everyone knows that the people of Babylon set great store by logic and symmetry. It was deemed inconsistent that lucky numbers should be reckoned in coinage and unlucky numbers in days and nights of imprisonment. Certain moralists pointed out that money does not always lead to happiness and that other forms of reward might be simpler.

A further concern swept the humbler neighbourhoods. Members of the college of priests, laying more bets than ever, were able to relish the thrills of impending terror or hope. Not so the poor, who knew, with inevitable and understandable envy, that they were barred from the much-touted delights of the lottery's fluctuations. The right and proper wish that rich and poor participate equally in the game sparked off an indignant protest, whose memory the years have not dimmed. A stubborn few failed to understand (or pretended to fail to understand) that a new order—an inescapable historical advance—was in the making. A slave stole a red ticket, which, when drawn, entitled him to have his tongue burned. This was the same penalty the law imposed for the theft of a lottery ticket. Some Babylonians argued that the man deserved the executioner's branding iron because he was a thief; others, more generous, because it was the luck of the draw.

There were riots, there was regrettable bloodshed, but in the end the will of Babylon's common people prevailed against that of the rich. The citizenry achieved its aims in full. First, it got the Company to take over the reins of power. (This unifying act was essential in view of the breadth and complexity of the operation's new scope.) Second, the citizenry managed to get the lottery made secret, gratis, and available to all. The sale of tickets for money was abolished. Now initiated into the mysteries of Bel, every free man was automatically entered in the sacred draws, which were held in the labyrinths of the god on each sixtieth night and which, until the next round, decided a man's fate. The possibilities were countless. A lucky draw could lead to promotion to the council of sages, to the arrest of a public or a personal enemy, or to a tryst in the hushed dark of a room with a woman who intrigues us but whom we never expected to see again; an unlucky draw, to mutilation, various types of disgrace, or death. Sometimes a single event—the murder of C in some low haunt, the mysterious deification of B—was the happy outcome of thirty or forty draws. Getting the combinations right was tricky, but it should be remembered that Company agents were (and are) shrewd and all-powerful. In many instances, the knowledge that certain lucky draws were simply a matter of chance would have lessened their attraction. To get round this difficulty, agents of the Company resorted to the power of suggestion and sorcery. Their manoeuvrings, their wiles, were secret. To find out everyone's intimate hopes and fears, they used spies and astrologers. Certain stone lions, a sacred privy called Qaphqa, cracks in a crumbling aqueduct—all these, according to popular belief, 'were pathways to the Company'. Both malicious and well-meaning people began informing on each other. Their reports, which were of varying reliability, were collected and filed away.

Unbelievably, the mutterings went on. The Company, with its usual prudence, did not reply directly. Instead, it chose to scrawl in the trash heap of a mask factory a brief explanation, which is now part of holy writ. This tenet affirmed that the lottery is an introduction of chance into the order of the world and that to accept error does not contradict but rather confirms chance. The doctrine further held that the lions and the sacred receptacle, although not unauthorised by the Company (which reserved the right to consult them), operated without official sanction.

This declaration allayed the fears of the public. It also gave rise to other consequences, perhaps not foreseen by its author. The statement profoundly changed the nature and conduct of the Company. I have little time left; we have been told that our ship is about to set sail, but I will try to explain things.

Strange as it may seem, no one so far had come up with a general theory of probability. Babylonians are little concerned with odds. They respect the dictates of chance, to which they hand over their lives, their hopes, and their wild panic, but it never occurs to my countrymen to look into the labyrinthine laws of chance or the revolving spheres that reveal them. Nevertheless, the semi-official statement I have referred to prompted much discussion of a juridico-mathematical cast. Out of some of this discussion came the following premise: If the lottery is a heightening of chance, a periodic infusion of chaos into the cosmos, would it not be better if chance intervened in all stages of the draw and not just one? Is it not absurd that if chance dictates someone's death the details of this death—

whether in obscurity or in the public eye, whether spanning an hour or a century—should not also be tied to chance? In the end, these quite reasonable reservations prompted a substantial reform, whose complexities (weighted by the practice of hundreds of years) only a handful of specialists understand. These complexities I shall try to sum up, albeit in a hypothetical way.

Let us imagine a first draw that sentences a man to death. To carry it out, we advance to a second draw, which comes up with, say, nine possible executioners. Of these, four may initiate a third draw, which will select the name of the actual executioner; two may replace the initial unlucky draw by a lucky one—the finding of treasure, for example; another may enhance the execution—either by bungling it or by enriching it with torture; the last two may refuse to carry out the sentence. This, in theory, is the plan. In reality, the number of draws is infinite. No decision is final, and all can branch out into others. The uninformed assume that infinite draws require infinite time, but the fact of the matter is that time is infinitely divisible, as the well-known parable of the hare and the tortoise teaches us. This infinitude ties in nicely with the sinuous gods of Chance and with the Heavenly Archetype of the Lottery so beloved of Platonists. Some garbled echo of our rituals seems to have reverberated along the Tiber. Aelius Lampridius, in his biography of Elagabalus, relates that the emperor wrote on seashells the lots that he intended for his guests, such that one would receive ten pounds of gold, another ten flies, a third ten dormice, a fourth ten bears. It should be remembered that Elagabalus was educated in Asia Minor among priests of the divinity whose name he bore.

There are also impersonal draws, with unspecific aims. One decrees that a Taprobane sapphire be flung into the waters of the Euphrates; another, that a bird be released from a tower roof; yet another, that once a century a grain of sand be removed from (or added to) the numberless grains on a beach. The consequences are sometimes terrible.

Under the Company's benevolent influence, our customs are permeated with chance. Anyone who purchases a dozen amphorae of Damascene wine will not be surprised if one of them contains a talisman or else a viper; the scribe who drafts a contract seldom fails to work in some piece of false information. I myself, in these hasty words, have distorted some of the splendour, some of the cruelty. Perhaps also some of the mysterious sameness. Our historians, who are the shrewdest in the world, have invented a method of adjusting chance. The mechanics of this method are widely known and (generally) reliable, although of course they are never disclosed without a pinch of falsehood. Aside from this, nothing is so tainted with fiction as the Company's history. A stone tablet excavated in a temple may refer to a draw made only the other day or to one made centuries ago. Not a volume is published without some difference in each copy. Scribes swear a secret oath to delete, insert, or change. Evasion is also employed.

The Company, with godlike restraint, shuns all publicity. As is only to be expected, its agents are covert, and the directives it continually (perhaps incessantly) issues are no different from those liberally dispensed by impostors. For who would boast of being a mere impostor? The drunkard who comes out with an absurd order, the dreamer who suddenly wakes and with his bare hands strangles the woman sleeping beside him—are they perhaps not carrying out one of the Company's secret decisions? These silent workings, so like those of God, give rise to all manner of speculation. One is the heinous suggestion that the Company has not existed for centuries and that the hallowed confusion in our lives is purely inherited, a tradition. Another deems the Company to be eternal and teaches that it will endure until the last trumpet, when the last remaining god will destroy the world.

Still another holds that the Company is everywhere at all times but that its influence is only over miniscule things—the call of a bird, the hues of rust or of dust, one's waking moments. Another, out of the mouths of masked heresiarchs, 'that it never existed and never will'. Another, equally base, reasons that to affirm or deny the existence of the phantom corporation is of no consequence, for Babylon itself is nothing more than one unending game of chance.

ERIS

86–90 Paul Street   265 Riverside Dr. #4G
London EC2A 4NE   New York, NY 10025

First published in 1941. English translation by Norman Thomas di Giovanni first published in *The Garden of Branching Paths* (2014).

The moral rights of the author and translator have been asserted.

ISBN 978-1-912475-96-4

All rights reserved. No part of this publication may be reproduced, stored in a retrieval system or transmitted in any form or by any means, electronic, mechanical, photocopying, recording or otherwise, without prior permission in writing from the Publisher.

eris.press